W9-BKG-020

Shall I Knit You a Hat?

a Christmas Yarn

OAK RIDGE PUBLIC LIBRARY
Civic Center
Oak Ridge, TN 37830

Kate Klise ✳ illustrated by **M. Sarah Klise**

Henry Holt and Company • New York

Henry Holt and Company, LLC
Publishers since 1866
115 West 18th Street
New York, New York 10011
www.henryholt.com

Henry Holt is a registered trademark of Henry Holt and Company, LLC
Text copyright © 2004 by Kate Klise
Illustrations copyright © 2004 by M. Sarah Klise
All rights reserved.
Distributed in Canada by H. B. Fenn and Company Ltd.

Library of Congress Catalog Card Number: 2003022497
Full Library of Congress Cataloging-in-Publication Data available at http://catalog.loc.gov/

ISBN 0-8050-7318-3 / EAN 978-0-8050-7318-8
First Edition—2004 / Designed by Patrick Collins
The artist used acrylic on Bristol board to create the illustrations for this book.
Printed in the United States of America on acid-free paper. ∞

1 3 5 7 9 10 8 6 4 2

JP Klise

1/2005 010542868 $17.00
Oak Ridge Public Library
Oak Ridge, TN 37830

Merry Christmas to Flora!
With love,
Aunt Sarah and Aunt Kate

"Oh dear. . . . Oh my. . . . Oh goodness me."
These were some of the things Mother Rabbit said
when she heard the news.

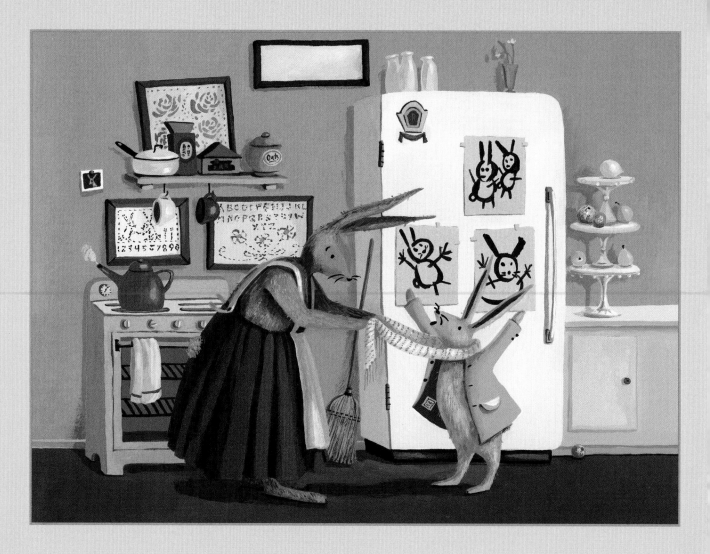

"A blizzard is moving this way," she told Little Rabbit as she tied his scarf the next morning. "It will start snowing on Christmas Eve and won't stop until the snow reaches the tallest tips of your ears."

"My ears?" asked Little Rabbit. "But that will be very cold."

"You're right," said Mother Rabbit. "Shall I knit you a hat to keep your ears warm?"

"Yes, please," said Little Rabbit. "A Christmas hat, just for me."

And so while Little Rabbit was at school, Mother
Rabbit knit and purled—*click click clack, click click
clack*—to the beat of the music on the radio.

That evening, Mother Rabbit tried the hat on Little
Rabbit. He stood very still while his mother made the
necessary adjustments. "Look how this hat shows off
your long, beautiful ears," said Mother Rabbit.

Little Rabbit agreed. He liked his new hat and wore
it even while he ate dinner. During dessert, he thought
of something. "What about our friends?" he asked.
"Shouldn't we make hats for them, too? We could give
them as Christmas presents!"

"Little Rabbit," said his mother, "that idea is so
delicious, it deserves a second piece of carrot cake."

The following day, they visited the horse, whose
mane Mother Rabbit measured while Little Rabbit
distracted him by telling a joke.

Next, they visited the goose, whose long neck they inspected without ruffling her feathers.

eggs toast beet

FRESH

sale

NEW!

CHESTNUTS

istletoe

They found their other friends at the market. Little Rabbit told them a story while Mother Rabbit secretly took measurements.

"That was a little sneaky," Mother Rabbit admitted
later that night as she and Little Rabbit ate dinner.
"Sneaky, yes," Little Rabbit agreed. "But necessary."

Mother Rabbit let Little Rabbit stay up very late that night—two hours past his bedtime—so he could help with the hats. The ideas were all his.

"The cat's hat must be smart and stylish, just like she is," Little Rabbit said. "The goose's hat will have a long scarf that wraps around her neck. The horse's hat should be part blanket so he can sleep in the snow. And the dog's hat must have an extra-long tail that looks pretty when it blows in the wind."

"And the deer's hat?" asked Mother Rabbit.
"The deer's hat will show off his lovely antlers,"
said Little Rabbit.

The next day was Christmas Eve. Late in the afternoon,
Little Rabbit and his mother pulled the gifts into town
on a sled.

When they arrived at the market, all their friends
gathered around to look at the beautifully wrapped gifts.

"Open your presents, please!" said Little Rabbit.
"We made them especially for you."

Little Rabbit held up a mirror. "See how beautiful
you look?"

And with that, the wind turned cold and the sky
became dark. The first snowflake fell.

"It's time, Little Rabbit," said Mother Rabbit. "We
must get back to our house."

"Oh dear. . . . Oh my. . . . Oh goodness me."
These were some of the things the friends said when
the snow began to fall . . . and fall . . . and fall.

"Just look how this clever hat keeps my head warm and dry," said the horse.

"Well, my long neck is perfectly comfortable," said the goose.

"My antlers have never been drier," said the deer.

"Have you noticed how pretty my tail looks when the wind blows?" asked the dog. "It's quite lovely, isn't it?"

Yes, they all agreed. It really was quite lovely.

"If we hurry," said the squirrel, "we can catch up with the Rabbits and thank them..."

. . .and they did.

"We are lucky," said the cat, "to have such nice friends as you Rabbits."

"Indeed!" chirped the squirrel. "This is the nicest, most thoughtful Christmas present anyone has ever given me."

But then, on the snowy sled ride home, Little
Rabbit had a terrible thought.

"Oh, no!" he said. "Tomorrow is Christmas, and
I forgot to make a present for *you*, Mother."

His mother squeezed him tight.

"Little Rabbit," she said, "being with you is the best gift of all."

Once they were safely home, the Rabbits celebrated
Christmas Eve with a carrot cake, warm from the oven.

OAK RIDGE PUBLIC LIBRARY
Civic Center
Oak Ridge TN 37830

JAN 1 2 2005